MW00416057

Sylvie
(Remembrances of Valois)

&

The Chimeras

Gérard de Nerval

Translated By Richard Robinson

Sunny Lou Publishing Company
Portland, Oregon, USA
http://www.sunnyloupublishing.com

Revised & Corrected: October 6, 2023 (A)

Original Publication Date: July 8, 2023

Translation Copyright © 2023 Richard Robinson.
All rights reserved.

ISBN: 978-1-955392-40-2

# # #

The translation from French of *Sylvie* is based on the D. Giraud, Libraire-Éditeur edition of *Filles du Feu*, Paris, 1854.

The translation from French of *The Chimeras* is based on the Ancienne Maison Michel Lévy Frères edition of *Oeuvres complètes de Gérard de Nerval, Tome 6: Poésies complètes, Paris, 1877.*

In the Appendix, the translation from French of an excerpt from "Gérard de Nerval" is from a biography by Henri Strentz in issue no. 44 of *Portraits d'hier,* a bi-monthly publication, Paris, January 1, 1911.

Contents

Muses

Where are our lovers?
They are in the grave!
They are happier there,
On a most beautiful stay!

They are next to the angels,
In a sky blue and broad,
And they sing the praises
Of the mother of God!

O pale fiancée!
O young virgin in flower!
Abandoned bonnie,
Whom sadnesses wither!

Profound eternity
Smiled in your eyes...
Spent torches of the world,
Shine again in the skies!

– Gérard de Nerval, *Odelettes*

Sylvie

Lost Night

I exited a theater where each evening I appeared in the loges dressed to the nines as a suitor. Sometimes the hall was full, sometimes it was empty. I was not interested in gazing down at a parterre peopled with thirty or so affected theater lovers, or at the other loges embellished with bonnets or outdated toilettes, – or even taking part in a vibrant and twittering room that was decorated at every level with flowery toilettes, sparkling jewelry, and radiant faces. Indifferent to the spectacle in the room, the one on the stage barely attracted my attention either, – except in the second or third scene of a dreary masterpiece of the time, when a well-known apparition brightened the empty space, breathing life, by a sigh or by a word, into those vain figures that surrounded me.

I felt alive in her presence, and she lived for me alone. Her smile filled me with infinite bliss; the vibration of her very gentle but strongly timbred voice made me shudder for joy and love. For me she possessed all the perfections, she responded to all my enthusiasms, all my caprices, – beautiful as the day in the lights of the stage that shone on her from below, pale as the night when the dimmed ramp left her illuminated by the lustrous rays from above and made her look more natural, shining in the shadow of her beauty alone, like the divine Hours who stand out from the dusky backgrounds of the frescoes in Herculaneum, with a star on their forehead!

For a year I had not even thought to inquire

about what she might have been like in other respects; I was afraid to upset the magic mirror that reflected her image to me, – and at most I had overheard some stories concerning not so much the actress, but the woman. I paid as little attention to them as I did to the gossip that might have circulated about the Princess d'Élide[1] or the Queen de Trébizonde,[2] – one of my uncles who had lived in the latter part of the eighteenth century (as he would have needed to, in order to be knowledgeable about it), warned me early on in life that actresses were not women, and that nature had forgotten to give them a heart. He was referring to those of that period, of course; but he had told me so many stories about his disillusionments and disappointments, and showed me so many portraits in ivory, charming medallions that he used since then to decorate snuffboxes, so many yellowed admission tickets, so many faded ribbons, while telling his story and giving me the definitive account, that I was accustomed to thinking ill of them all, without considering that the times had changed.

We were living at that time in a strange epoch, like those ordinarily following revolutions or the fall of great reigns. There was no longer that heroic gallantry as under the Fronde, or the elegant and ornate vice as under the Regency, or the skepticism and mad orgies of the Directory; there was a mixture of activity, hesitation, and indolence, brilliant utopias, philo-

---

[1]Princess d'Élide: perhaps in reference to an opera entitled *La princesse d'Élide,* by Molière (AD 1622-1673).

[2]The Queen de Trébizonde: perhaps in reference to the opera bouffe entitled *La princesse de Trébizonde,* by Jacques Offenbach (AD 1819-1880).

sophical or religious aspirations, vague enthusiasms, together with a certain Renaissance of instincts; of boredom for passed discord, of uncertain expectations, – something akin to the epoch of Peregrinus[3] and Apuleius.[4] Material man longed for the bouquet of roses that was supposed to regenerate him through the hands of the beautiful Isis; the eternally young and pure goddess appeared to us at night, and made us ashamed of the time we had wasted during the day. But ambition was not a characteristic of our age, and the avid scramble that was made then for positions of power and honor distanced us from other possible spheres of activity. We had no other resort than the ivory tower of poets, where we always climbed higher and higher in order to isolate ourselves from the crowd. At those elevated vantage points where our masters guided us, we finally breathed the pure air of solitudes, we drank forgetfulness in the golden cup of legends, we were drunk on poetry and love. Love, alas! assuming indistinct shapes of pink and blue tints, metaphysical phantoms! Seen at close range, a real woman revolted our ingenuousness; she needed to appear like a queen or a goddess, and be unapproachable above all.

Some among us, however, did not take too kindly to those Platonic paradoxes, and through our revitalized dreams of Alexandria they sometimes agitated the subterranean gods' torch which, with its trail of sparks, momentarily lights up the darkness. It is in

---

[3]Peregrinus: Peregrinus Proteus (AD 95-165), a Greek Cynic Philosopher.

[4]Apuleius: a Numidian-Roman writer and Platonist philosopher (AD 124-170), the author of *The Golden Ass*.

this way that, on leaving the theatre with the bitter sadness that a vanished dream leaves behind, I sought out the company of the men of a circle where one dined in great numbers, and where every melancholy gave way before the inexhaustible verve of some vibrant, lively, stormy, sublime sometimes, minds, – such as are always found in times of renewal or decadence, and whose discussions were raised to the point where the most timid amongst us went to look out the windows and see if the Huns, the Turks, or the Cossacks had not come finally in order to cut short the arguments of these rhetors and sophists.

"Let us drink, let us love, – that is wisdom!" Such was the one and only opinion of the youngest members. One of them said to me: "It's been quite a while since I've run into you in the same theater, and I attend every show. *Which actress* do you come for?"

Which actress?... It hadn't occurred to me that one could go there for any *other*. I gave him a name, however. – "Ah, well!" said my friend indulgently, "over there you will see the lucky man who has just escorted her, and who, faithful to the laws of our circle, will go and look for her again but not until after nightfall perhaps."

Without too much emotion, I turned my eyes toward the indicated person. He was a young man, well dressed, with a pale and nervous face, having suitable manners and eyes imbued with melancholy and gentleness. He tossed some gold coins onto the table of whist and lost them with an indifference. "What does it matter to me," I said, "whether it be him or anyone else? She had to have someone, and he appears as good as any for her to have chosen." "And you?" "And me? It's an image I chase after, a reflection, nothing more."

I passed through the reading room on my way out, and, automatically I glanced at a newspaper. It was, I believe, in order to consult the prices of the Stock market. In the ruins of my opulence there remained a rather large sum in foreign securities. Rumor had it that, although neglected for a long time, they had been rediscovered; – this occurred following a change of government. The funds had already risen so high that I found myself a rich man again.

One thought alone passed through my head, from this change in situation: that the woman I had loved for so long was mine if I wanted her. My ideal was within grasp. Was it just another illusion, a printing error that was mocking me? But other newspapers printed the same thing. The amount of wealth I had just acquired loomed before my eyes like Moloch's golden statue. "What would he say now, that young man of earlier, if I went to take his place beside the woman whom he had just left all alone?..." I shivered at the thought of it, and my pride revolted.

No! It does not work like that, it is not at my age that one kills love with gold: I will not be a corrupter. Besides, this is an idea from another time. Also, what tells me that that woman is venal? My gaze passed vaguely over the newspaper that I continued holding in my hands, and I read these two lines: "*Country Celebration of the Bouquet*. Tomorrow, the archers of Senlis must yield the bouquet to those of Loisy." These words, so very simple, awoke in me a

new series of impressions: it was a memory of the
countryside that I had so long forgotten, a distant
echo of the naïve celebrations of my youth. The horn
and drum resounded in the distant hamlets and in the
woods; girls wove garlands and, while singing,
awarded the bouquets decorated with ribbons. A
heavy cart, pulled by bulls, received these presents
during its passage, and we, children of the villages,
we formed the cortege with our bows and arrows,
bearing the title of chevalier, – without realizing at
the time that we were repeating from a time immemo-
rial a Druidic feast that had survived monarchies and
new religions.

Adrienne

I regained my room and took to my bed but could not find any rest there. Plunged in a half-somnolence, I saw all my youthful memories pass before my eyes. That state wherein the spirit still resists the bizarre combinations of dream often permits one to see the most salient scenes of a long period of life compressed into several minutes.

I represented to myself a chateau from the time of Henry IV with its pointed roofs covered in grey slate tiles and its reddish front with crenelated corners of yellow stone, a large green square framed by elms and linden trees where the setting sun pierced the foliage with its enflamed rays. Several girls danced in a round on the grass, singing old songs passed down by their mothers, and in so naturally pure a French that one felt as though one were really alive in the old Valois countryside where for more than a thousand years the heart of France beat.

I was the only boy in that round dance where I had led my, as yet, very young companion, Sylvie, a girl from the neighboring hamlet, so lively and fresh with her black eyes, her regular profile, and her lightly suntanned skin!... I loved no one but her, I saw no one but her, – until then! I had scarcely noticed in the round dance where we were dancing, a tall, beautiful blonde girl, who went by the name of Adrienne. All of a sudden, following the rules of the dance, Adrienne found herself alone with me in the middle of the circle. Our heights were equal. They told us to give each other a kiss, and the dance and the chorus turned more lively than ever. On giving her that kiss, I could not stop myself from pressing her hand. The long, curled rings of her golden hair brushed my cheeks. From that moment onwards, an unknown trouble took hold of me.The beautiful girl was supposed to sing in order to be allowed to rejoin the dance. We all sat around her and immediately, in a fresh and penetrating, slightly husky voice, like those of the girls of this foggy area, she sang one of those ancient ballads full of melancholy and love, which always told of the misfortunes of a princess locked in a tower by the will of her father who punishes her for having loved. The melody was punctuated at the end of each stanza by those quavering trills that young voices know so well how to make, when they imitate by a modulated shiver the trembling voices of their grandmothers.

As she sang, the shadows descended from the tall trees, and a nascent moonlight fell on her alone, standing out from our attentive circle. She fell silent, and nobody dared break the silence. The lawn was covered in a thin, condensed vapor that collected in clear droplets on the tips of the grass blades. We thought we were in paradise. I got up finally, running to the chateau's flowerbed where the laurels were found, planted in large earthenware vases that were painted monochrome. I brought back two branches, which were braided together into a crown and tied with a ribbon. I put that ornament on Adrienne's head, where the lustrous leaves shone in her blonde hair in the pale beams of moonlight. She looked like Dante's Beatrice, smiling at the poet wandering on the outskirts of holy abodes.

Adrienne rose finally. Assuming her slender height, she bade us a gracious farewell, and returned home, running into the chateau. She was, we were told, the granddaughter of one of the descendants of a family related to the ancient kings of France; Valois blood ran in her veins. For that day of celebration, she was allowed to participate in our games; we would never see her again, for on the morrow she returned to the convent where she was a boarder.

When I returned to Sylvie's side, I noticed tears in her eyes. The crown placed by my hands on the beautiful singer's head was the reason for her tears. I offered to go and get another crown for her, but she said that she had no desire for one, not deserving it. I tried in vain to defend myself, but she remained silent as I escorted her back to her parents.

Having been recalled to Paris to resume my studies, I carried with me that dual image of a tender friendship sadly broken, – and of an impossible and vague love, the source of painful thoughts that the philosophy of college was powerless to calm.

The image of Adrienne alone remained triumphant, – a mirage of glory and beauty, which comforted or shared my hours of bitter study. During the following year's vacations, I learned that the beautiful girl whom I barely knew had been consecrated by her family to the religious life.

Resolution

Everything was explained to me in that half-dreamt memory. That vague and hopeless love conceived for a woman of the theater, who received me every evening at the hour of showtime, which left me only at the time of sleep, had its germ in the memory of Adrienne, a night flower opening in the moonlight, rosy and blonde phantom gliding over the green grass half-bathed in white vapors. The resemblance of a face forgotten after all these years painted itself in my mind with singular clarity from that moment forward; it was a pastel stumped by time that created a picture, similar to those old sketches by ancient masters admired in a museum, whose dazzling original can be found elsewhere.

To love a nun in the guise of an actress!... as if she were the same person! – it is enough to drive a man crazy! It was a fatal attraction where the unknown lures you like a will-o'-the-wisp fleeting over the rushes standing in stagnant water... Let us regain our footing in reality.

And Sylvie whom I loved so much, why did I forget her for all these three years?... She was a fine, pretty girl, and the most beautiful girl in Loisy!

She exists, she does, good and pure of heart without any doubt. Once again I see her window where vine branches interlace with the roses', a cage of warblers suspended to the left; I hear the sound of her sonorous spindles and her favorite song:

La belle était assise
Près du ruisseau coulant...[5]

She still waits for me... Who would have married her? She is so poor!

In her village, and in those that surround it, good peasants in blouses, with rude hands, thin faces, suntanned complexions! She loved me alone, me, the little Parisian, when I went to see my poor uncle, who is now dead, near Loisy. Over the past three years, acting like a little lord, I have dissipated the modest capital that he left me, which might have lasted a lifetime. With Sylvie, I would have conserved it. Luck has returned some of it to me. There is still time.

What is she doing at this hour of the day? She sleeps... No, she does not sleep; today is the celebration of the bow, the one celebration of the year when villagers dance through the night. She is at the festival...

What time is it?

I do not have a watch.

In the midst of all the brac-à-brac splendors that I was wont to collect at this epoch in order to remodel an apartment in the local color of bygone days, there shined with particular brightness one of those tortoiseshell pendule clocks from the Renaissance, whose gilt dome surmounted by the figure of Time was held up by caryatids in the style of the Medicis, sitting in turn on half-rearing horses. A historical rep-

---

[5]*La belle... coulant*: French for "The beautiful girl remained seated/Beside the moving stream..."

resentation of Diana, leaning on her stag, is in bas-re-lief under the dial, where the enameled numbers of the hour are spread out on a nielloed background. The mechanism's movement, excellent of course, had not been remounted for two centuries. It was not for telling the hours that I had bought this pendule in Touraine.

I went downstairs to the see the concierge. His cuckoo struck one o'clock in the morning. In four hours, I told myself, I can arrive at the ball in Loisy. There were still in the place du Palais-Royal five or six fiacres stationed there for the regulars of circles and gambling houses: "To Loisy!" I said to the first one I came across. "Where's that?" "Near Senlis, eight leagues from here." "I will take you to the post chaise," said the driver, less concerned than me.

What a sad journey at night is that road to Flanders, which only becomes beautiful when one reaches the zone of the forests! Always those two mo-notonous lines of trees that grimace with vague ex-pressions; beyond that, squares of verdure and turned earth, bordered on the left by the bluish hills of Mont-morency, Écouen, Luzarches. Here is Gonesse, the people's burg filled with memories of the Catholic League and the Fronde...

Beyond Louvres a ways is a road bordered by apple trees where I have on multiple occasions seen flowers shining in the night like stars of the earth: it was the shortest route by which to reach the hamlets. While the carriage climbs the slopes, let us go over some of the memories of the period when I came here so often.

A Voyage to Cythera

A few years had passed: the time when I had met Adrienne in front of the chateau was already a child-hood memory and nothing more. I happened to be in Loisy at the moment of the patronal festival. I went once again to join the chevaliers of the bow, taking part in the company that I had taken part in before. The young folk belonging to the old families who still possess many of those chateaus lost in the forests there, which have suffered more at the hands of time than revolutions, had organized the celebration. From Chantilly, Compiégne, and Senlis, joyous cavalcades hastened to the festival and took their places in the rustic cortege of the companies of the bow. After the long promenade through villages and burgs, after the mass at church, competitions and the distribution of prizes, the victors had been invited to a meal that was given on an island shaded by poplars and linden trees, in the middle of one of the lakes fed by the Nonette and Thève rivers. Barques decked with flags carried us to the island, – whose choice had been determined by the existence of an oval temple with columns that was supposed to serve as the feast hall. There, as at Ermenonville, the country is riddled with these small edifices from the end of the eighteenth century, when millionaire philosophers were inspired in their de-signs by the dominant taste of the period. I strongly believe that this temple must have been originally dedicated to Urania. Three columns had given way, bringing down with them in their fall a part of the ar-chitrave; but someone had swept up the debris from the interior of the hall and suspended garlands between the standing columns; they had spruced up that modern ruin, which belonged to the paganism of Boufflers or Chaulieu more than to that of Horace.

The crossing of the lake was designed perhaps to recall the *Voyage to Cythera* by Watteau. Our modern costumes by themselves upset the illusion. The immense bouquet of the feast, taken from the cart that carried it, had been placed on a large barque; the cortege of young women dressed in white who accompanied it according to the custom had taken their places on the banks, and that graceful *sacred procession* renewed from bygone days was reflected in the calm waters of the lake that separated it from the banks of the island, so vermillion in the light of evening with its brushwood, colonnades, and clear foliage. All the barques landed after a small amount of time. The basket, ceremoniously carried, occupied the center of the table, and each person took his place around it, the most favored boys sitting beside the young women: for that it sufficed to be known by their parents. This was the reason that I found myself next to Sylvie. Her brother had already caught up with me at the celebration and reprimanded me for not having paid a visit to his family after such a long time. I excused myself because of my studies, which held me in Paris, and assured him that I had come with no other intention. "No, it's me who he forgot," said Sylvie. "We are people of the village, and Paris is so superior!" I wanted to give her a kiss to stop her from talking; but she continued to give me the cold shoulder, and her brother had to intervene for her to offer me her cheek with an indifferent air. I took no pleasure in that kiss which many others had obtained the favor of, for in this patriarchal region where one greets every man who passes, a kiss is nothing more than a courtesy between well-bred people.

The organizers of the feast had arranged for a surprise. At the end of the meal, we saw a wild swan rise up from the bottom of the huge basket, captive under the flowers until then, which with its strong wings, lifting the network of garlands and crowns, and finished by dispersing them in all directions. While it was rising joyously towards the last glimmers of the sun, we caught by chance the crowns, which each one of us used to decorate the head of his neighbor with. I was lucky enough to catch one of the most beautiful crowns, and Sylvie, smiling, let herself be kissed this time more tenderly than before. I understood that I had erased in this way the memory of another time. I admired her this time with all my heart, she had become so beautiful! She was no longer that little village girl whom I had looked down on in favor of an older girl, more developed in the world's graces. Everything about her had improved: the charm of her dark eyes, so seductive since childhood, had become irresistible; under her arched eyebrows, her smile, revealing immediately the regular and placid features of her face, had something Athenian about it. I admired her physiognomy worthy of antique art amidst the crumpled little faces of her companions. Her gracefully elongated hands, her arms which had grown white and filled out, her perky waist, made her look quite different from before. I could not help telling her how different she looked now, hoping to cover up my old and fleeting infidelity.

What is more, everything was working in my favor: her brother's friendship, the charming impression of that feast, the evening hour, and the very location where, by a fantasy full of good taste, they had reproduced an image of the gallant solemnities of yesteryear. As much as we possibly could, Sylvie and I escaped from the dance in order to talk about our memories of childhood and to admire, while dreaming together, the reflections of the sky on the shadows and in the water. Sylvie's brother had to pull us away from that contemplation saying that it was time to go back to the village where their parents lived, rather far away.

The Village

It was at Loisy, in the ancient guardhouse. I escorted her there, then I returned to Montagny, where I was staying at my uncle's. On leaving the road behind, in order to cross through the small wood that separated Loisy from Saint-S***, it was not long before I entered into a deep *path* that runs beside the Ermenonville forest; I was expecting finally to meet the walls of a convent that I needed to follow along for a quarter of a league. The moon was hiding behind the clouds, from one moment to the next, illuminating difficultly the dark-gray rocks and heather that were growing thicker under my feet. To the right and left, the limits of the forest without paths through it, and always before me those druidic rocks of the country that kept alive the memory of the sons of Armen exterminated by the Romans! From the heights of those sublime rock heaps I saw the distant lakes breaking up like mirrors on the foggy plain, being unable to distinguish the one even where the feast had taken place.

The air was warm and fragrant; I resolved to go no farther and to wait for morning, lying down on the tufts of heather. On awakening, I gradually recognized the nearby reference points that I had missed during the night. To my left, I saw coming into focus the long line of walls of the convent of Saint-S***, then the other side of the valley, the butte Gens-d'Armes, with the smashed-in ruins of the ancient Carolingian residence. Next to it, above the tufts of wood, the lofty tumbledowns of the Abbey of Theirs stood out against the horizon with their stretches of wall pierced by trefoils and ogives. Beyond that, the Gothic manor of Pontarmé, surrounded by water as before, soon reflected the first light of day, while I saw to the south the tall donjon of the Tournelle standing high, and the four towers of Bertrand-Fosse on the first hills of Montméliant.

That night had been sweet to me, and I thought only about Sylvie; however, the sight of the convent made me think for an instant that it was the one where Adrienne lived. The morning bells were still ringing in my ears and had clearly been what woke me. An instant later, I thought of casting a glance over the convent walls by climbing to the highest point of the rocks; but on greater reflection, I refrained from that like a profanation. The growing light chased that vain memory of her from my thoughts and left no more than Sylvie's rosy traits. "Let's go wake her," I said to myself, and I took up the road to Loisy again.

Here is the village at the end of the path that borders the forest: eighteen thatched cottages whose exterior walls are festooned with climbing grape and roses. The early morning spinners, wearing red hand-kerchiefs on their head, work in a group in front of a farmhouse. Sylvie is not among them. She is almost a young lady, now that she produces fine lace, while her parents have remained good villagers. I climbed the stairs to her room without giving notice to any-one; already risen for a long time now, Sylvie was working the bobbins of her lace, which clacked with a soft sound against the green square that she held on her knees. "There you are, lazy bones," she said with a divine smile, "I am sure that you just got out of bed!" I told her how I spent the night without sleep, my lost wanderings through the woods and among the rocks. She really wanted to grumble at me for an instant. "If you're not tired, I am going to make you do more walking. We are going to visit my great aunt in Othys." I had barely responded when she got up joyously, arranged her hair in front of the mirror, and put on a rustic straw hat. Her eyes were beaming with innocence and joy. We left, following the banks of the Thève, through the fields planted with daisies and gold buttons, then along the banks of the Saint-Laurent, crossing the stream sometimes, and through the thickets, in order to shorten the route. The blackbirds whistled in the trees, and the titmice fluttered joyously out of the bushes that were brushed by us as we walked.

At times, under our steps, we came across the periwinkle that was so dear to Rousseau, opening their blue corollas among those long branches of coupled leaves, modest creepers that stopped my companion's furtive feet. Indifferent to the memories of the Genevan philosopher, she sought fragrant strawberries here and there, while I spoke to her about the *Nouvelle Héloïse*, from which I recited several passages by heart. "Is it nice?" she asked. "It's sublime." "Is it better than Auguste Lafontaine?" "It's tenderer." "Oh! good," she said, "I must read it then." I will ask my brother to bring a copy back for me the next time he goes to Senlis." And I continued to recite fragments from *Héloïse* while Sylvie gathered strawberries.

Othys

On exiting the wood, we ran across large tufts of fox-glove; she made an enormous bouquet of it, saying to me: "It's for my aunt; she will be so happy to have these beautiful flowers in her room." We had no more than one end of the plain to cross before arriving at Othys. The village steeple pointed above the bluish hills that extend from Montméliant to Dammartin. The Thève could be heard again between the sand-stone and the rocks, becoming narrower in the neigh-borhood of its source, where it settles in the meadow, forming a small lake in the middle of gladiolas and irises. Soon we reached the first houses. Sylvie's aunt inhabited a small cottage built of sandstones of vari-ous sizes that was covered by trellises of hops and woodbine; she lived alone on several hectares of land that people from the village cultivated for her since the death of her husband. Her niece's arrival brought warmth into the house. "Good morning, aunt! Here we are!" said Sylvie, "We are famished!" She kissed her tenderly, put two bunches of flowers into her arms, then she thought to introduce me finally, say-ing, "This is my sweetheart!"

It was my turn to kiss the aunt, who said: "He's nice... So he's a blond!..." "He has nice, fine hair," said Sylvie. "That won't last," said the aunt; "But you have lots of time ahead of you both, and you who are a brunette, that goes well together." "We need to make breakfast, aunt" said Sylvie. And she went to look in the cupboards, on the hutch, finding milk, brown bread, sugar, setting the plates on the ta-

ble and the glazed earthenware dishes with flower
patterns on them and patterns of roosters with bright-
colored plumage. A porcelain bowl from Creil, full of
milk, with strawberries floating in it, was at the center
of the table, and after having deprived the garden of
several handfuls of cherries and currants, she arranged two vases of flowers at either end of the table-
cloth. But the aunt had said these beautiful words:
"All that is only desert. Now let me take care of it."
And she got down the frying pan and threw a faggot
into the tall fireplace. "I don't want you to touch it"
she said to Sylvie, who wanted to help her; you'll
spoil your pretty fingers that make the most beautiful
lace in Chantilly! You gave me some, and I know
what I'm talking about." "Ah! Yes, aunt!... By the
way, if you have any ancient morsels, that would
serve as models." "Ah, well! go look upstairs," said
the aunt, "there's something maybe in my chest of
drawers." "Give me the keys," replied Sylvie. "Bah!"
said the aunt, "the drawers are open." "That's not
true! there is one that is always locked." And while
the good woman cleaned the pan, after having put it
into the fire, Sylvie was untangling from the pendants
of her belt a small key in worked steel that she
showed me triumphantly.

I followed her, quickly climbing the wooden
stairs that led to the bedroom. O sacred youth! oh sacred old age! – who would have thought to tarnish the
purity of a first love in this sanctuary of faithful memories? The portrait of a young man from the good old
days was smiling with his dark eyes and his pinkish
mouth, in an oval gilt frame, suspended at the head of
the rustic bed. He was wearing the gamekeeper's uni-

form of the House of Condé; his half-martial attitude, his ruddy and benevolent face, his pure forehead under the powdered hair, enhanced this pastel, mediocre perhaps, with the charms of youth and simplicity. Some modest artist invited to princely hunts had applied himself as best he could to draw this portrait, as well as that of his young wife whom one saw in another medallion, attractive, mischievous, slender in her half-open bodice and its ladder of ribbons, teasing a bird perched on her finger. She was nonetheless the same good old woman who was cooking that very moment, hunched over the fire in the hearth. It made me think of the faeries at the Théâtre des Funambules who hide an attractive face under their wrinkled masks, which they only reveal at the denouement when the temple of Love appears with its rotating sun shooting out rays of magical fire. "O good aunt," I exclaimed, "how pretty you were!" "And me?" said Sylvie, who had succeeded in opening the famous drawer. She had found in it a large dress in taffetas flambé, that screeched when one of its folds was rubbed. "I want to see if it fits me," she said. "Ah! I'll look like an old faery!"

"The legendary faery, forever young!..." I said to myself. And already Sylvie had unfastened her printed calico dress and let it fall to her feet. The old aunt's fabric dress fit Sylvie's slender waist to a T; she asked me to fasten it up. "Oh! the flat sleeves, how ridiculous!" she said. And yet the lace-garnished clogs beautifully complimented her bare arms, while her bosom was enhanced in the pure corsage with its yellowed tulle and old-fashioned ribbons, which had squeezed the aunt's vanished charms not often

enough. "What's taking you! You don't know how to
fasten a dress?" Sylvie said to me. She looked like the
girl in Greuze's *L'Accordée de Village*. "We need
powder," I said. We went to find some. She rum-
maged through the drawers again. Oh! What trea-
sures! What fragrance! Everything sparkled, everything was shimmering in vivid colors and a subdued
bling! Two slightly broken, mother-of-pearl fans,
cardboard boxes with Chinese designs on them, an
amber necklace and a thousand trinkets, amongst
which two small slippers stood out, made of white
drugget and Irish diamonds inlaid in the buckles!
"Oh! I want to try them on," Sylvie said, "if only I
can find embroidered socks!"

A moment later we were unrolling the silk,
pink-and-green checkered socks; but the aunt's voice,
accompanied by a banging of the pan, called us back
to reality. "Let's go!" said Sylvie, and no matter what
I said, she would not permit me to help her put her
shoes back on. But the aunt had just poured the con-
tents of the pan onto a plate, a slice of fried lard with
eggs. Sylvie's voice called me back. "Dress, hurry!"
she said, and still dressed in the old outfit herself, she
showed me the wedding outfit of the gamekeeper on
the commode. In an instant, I transformed myself into
a husband of another century. Sylvie was waiting for
me at the top of the stairs, and we descended together
holding each other's hand. The aunt let out a cry and
turned away: "O my children!" she said, and she began crying, then she smiled through the tears. We
were the picture of her youth – a cruel and charming
apparition! We sat down beside her, emotional and
serious almost, but then our gaiety returned because,

after the first moment had passed, the good aunt's only thought was about the solemn celebrations of her wedding day. She even recalled the antiphonal songs, customary back then, that were sung alternately from one end of the nuptial table to the other, and the naïve epithalamium that accompanied the newlyweds on going home after the dance. We repeated those strophes with their simple rhythms, with the hiatuses and assonances typical of the period; amorous and flowery, like the Song of Songs; – we were husband and wife for one entire beautiful summer morning.

Chaâlis

It is four o'clck in the morning; the road plunges in a dip in the terrain; it climbs again. The carriage is going to pass Orry, then La Chapelle. To the left, there is a route that skirts the Forest of Halatte. It is through it that Sylvie's brother one evening brought me in his carriole to a regional solemnity. It was, I believe, St. Bartholomew's Eve. Through the forest, over the overgrown ways, his small horse flew as if to a sabbath. We regained pavement at Mont-Lévêque, and a few minutes later we stopped at the guardhouse, before the ancient abbey de Chaâlis. Chaâlis, – another memory!

That old retreat of emperors no longer offers admirers anything more than the ruins of its cloister with its byzantine arcades, the last row of which stands out still over the ponds, – forgotten remainder of the pious foundations contained in those domains that formerly were called the sharecrops of Charlemagne. The religion in this area isolated from the traffic of roads and cities conserved particular traces of the long sojourn that cardinals of the House of Este had made there in the time of the Medici: its attributes and its usages have still something of gallantry and the poetic about them, and one breathes in a fragrance of rebirth under the arches of the chapels with their fine ribs, decorated by Italian artists. The figures of saints and angels stand out in pink on the vaults painted in a tender blue color, with touches of pagan allegory that make one think of the sentimentalities of Petrarch and the fabulous mysticism of Colonna.

We were intruders, Sylvie's brother and I, into the particular celebration that was taking place that night. A person of very illustrious birth, who possessed that domain then, had had the idea of inviting several families of the region to a sort of allegorical representation wherein several pensioners of the neighboring convent were supposed to take part. It was not a reminiscence of Saint-Cyr's tragedies, it harked back to the first lyrical attempts imported into France at the time of the Valois. What I saw put on was something of a mystery of olden times. The costumes, made of long robes, varied only in color: azure, hyacinth, or aurora. The scene took place between angels, over the debris of that destroyed world. Each voice sang of the splendors of that spent globe, and the angel of death defined the causes of its destruction. A spirit climbed out of the abyss, a flaming sword in hand, and convoked others to come and admire the glory of Christ, the harrower of hell. This spirit, it was Adrienne transfigured by her costume, as she was already by vocation. The gilt cardboard nimbus that girt her angelic head appeared to us quite naturally like a circle of light; her voice had gained in force and carry, and the infinite flourish of the Italian song embellished the harsh phrases of a pompous recitative with their bird warblings.

As I go over these details, I have to ask myself whether they are real, or whether I did not dream them. Sylvie's brother was a little tipsy that evening. We had paused for a few instants at the guardhouse, where, what really struck me, was a heraldic swan on the gate and then, inside, the tall walnut-sculpted wardrobes, a grandfather clock, and honorary bow-

and-arrow trophies above a red and green paper target. A bizarre dwarf, wearing a Chinese hat, holding a bottle in one hand and a ring in the other, seemed to invite the shooters to aim straight. This dwarf, I firmly believe, was made of cut sheetmetal. But the appearance of Adrienne, is it as real as all these details and the incontestable existence of the abbey of Chaâlis? But it was actually the son of the guard who had introduced us into the room where the representation took place; we were near the door, behind a numerous company who were seated and deeply moved. It was the feast day of Saint Bartholomew, particularly tied to the memory of the Medici, whose heraldic arms placed beside those of the House of Este decorated those old walls... That memory is an obsession perhaps! Fortunately, the carriage has now come to a stop on the way to Plessis; I escape the world of reveries, and I have no more than a quarter of an hour of walking to do before gaining Loisy via overgrown routes.

The Loisy Dancehall

I entered the Loisy Dancehall at that still melancholic and sweet hour when the lights begin to fade and tremble with the approach of day. The linden trees, dark closer to the ground, had a bluish tint at their tops. The rustic flute no longer competed so strenuously with the nightingale's trills. Everyone looked pale, and in the thinning groups I barely recognized any faces. Finally, I noticed tall Lise, a friend of Sylvie's. She gave me an embrace. "Long time no see, Parisian!" she said. "Oh! yes, a long time." "And you show up at this hour!" "By post chaise." "And not too fast!" "I wanted to see Sylvie; is she still at the ball?" "She only leaves at morning; she so loves to dance."

In an instant, I was beside her. Her face looked tired; however her dark eyes shone as usual with the Athenian smile of before. A young man was standing next to her. She made him a sign to him that she would pass on the following quadrille. He took his leave while saying goodbye.

Morning was beginning to break. We exited the dancehall, holding each other's hand. The flowers in Sylvie's loosened hair were drooping their heads; the bouquet of her corsage was also dropping petals onto the crumpled lace of her expert handiwork. I offered to accompany her home. The sun had fully risen by now, but the atmosphere was still somber. The Thève gurgled on our left, leaving stagnant eddies of water at its bends where yellow and white water lilies bloomed, where the frail embroidery of water stars sparkled like daisies. The plains were covered in swaths and stacks of hay, whose odor went to my head without intoxicating me, as the fresh scent of the woods and the flowering thickets of thornbushes used to do.

We did not recall having walked this way before. "Sylvie," I said to her, "you don't love me anymore!" She sighed. "My friend," she said to me, "there must be a reason; things don't always go as we wish them to in life. You spoke to me before about the *Nouvelle Héloïse*; I read it, and I shuddered at first when coming across this phrase: 'Every girl who reads this book will be lost.' But I passed beyond, trusting my reason. Do you remember the day when we dressed up in the my aunt's wedding outfits?... The illustrations in the book showed lovers in the old costumes of the past as well, and you were Saint-Preux for me, and I saw myself in Julie. Ah! if only you had come back then! But you were, it is said, in Italy. You must have seen girls there much more beautiful than me!" "Not a one, Sylvie, who has your expression and the pure traits of your face. You are an ancient nymph and do not realize it. Besides, the woods in these parts are just as beautiful as those in the Roman countryside. There are magnificent masses of granite here no less sublime than there, and a waterfall that falls from the a height like that of Terni. I saw nothing there that I have not seen here."

"And Paris?" she said.

"In Paris..."

I shook my head without responding.

Suddenly, I thought of the empty image that had led me astray for so long.

"Sylvie," I said, "let's stop here, okay?"

I threw myself at her feet; I confessed, while shedding warm tears, my irresolutions, my caprices; I evoked the fatal specter that was running through my life.

"Save me!" I added, "I return to you forever."

She turned towards me with a softened gaze...

At this moment our conversation was interrupted by violent outbursts of laughter. It was Sylvie's brother who rejoined us with that hearty rustic gaiety, the inevitable consequence of a night of celebrating, which numerous refreshments had amplified beyond measure. He called out to the gallant of the dancehall, lost in the distant thornbushes and who did not take long to catch up with us. This fellow was hardly any more solid on his feet than his companion, he appeared even more embarrassed by the sight of a Parisian than that of Sylvie. His candid face, his deference mixed with embarrassment, prevented me from being upset with him for having been the dancer for whom she had stayed so late at the celebration. I did not consider him much of a danger.

"We should get on home," Sylvie said to her brother. "See you soon!" she said to me, offering me her cheek.

The sweetheart was not offended.

Ermenonville

I had no desire to sleep. I went to Montagny to see the house of my uncle again. A great sadness overcame me when I saw the yellow facade and green shutters. It all seemed to be in the same condition as before; only, I had to go to the farmer's house to get the key to the door. Once the shutters were open, I saw again with tender feelings the old furniture kept in the same state as before, and which someone dusted from time to time, – the tall walnut armoire, two Flemish tableaux said to be the work of an ancient painter, our ancestor; big prints in the style of Boucher, and an entire framed series of engravings of *Émile* and the *Nouvelle Héloïse*, by Moreau; on the table, a stuffed dog that I had known when it was alive, old companion of my walks through the woods, the last pug perhaps, for it belonged to that lost race.

"As for the parroquet," said the farmer, "it's still alive; I brought it home with me."

The garden presented a magnificent tableaux of wild vegetation. I recognized, in a corner, a child's garden where I had worked the soil formerly. I entered the side room where the small bookcase full of select books could still be seen, old friends of the man who was no longer here, and on the bureau several antique objects found in his garden, vases, Roman medallions, a local collection that made him happy.

"Let's go see the parroquet," I said to the farmer.

The parroquet asked for lunch just as it did in better days, and it looked at me with that round eye, bordered by wrinkled skin, which reminds one of the experienced look of old men.

Filled with the sad thoughts that this long-delayed return to such beloved places stirred up in me, I felt the need to see Sylvie again, the one person, young and still alive, who tied me to this region. I took the road back to Loisy. It was the middle of the day; everyone was sleeping, tired from the celebration. The idea came to me to distract myself by a walk to Ermenonville, at a distance of one league by forest path. The summer weather was gorgeous. I took an immediate pleasure in the freshness of that path which seemed like a lane through a park. The big oaks of a uniform green color were only varied in the white trunks of the birches with their quaking foliage. The birds were quiet, and I heard only the sound of the woodpecker striking the trees in order to hollow out its nest. At one point, I almost got lost, because some of the signposts announcing the various paths had had their characters effaced. Finally, leaving the *Desert* to the left, I arrived at the roundabout of the dance, where the old people's bench still subsisted. All the memories of philosophical antiquity, resuscitated by the ancient possessor of the domain, came crowding back to me before this picturesque reproduction of *Anacharsis* and *Émile.*

When I saw the waters of the lake shimmering through the branches of the willow trees and hazel trees, I immediately recognized a place where my uncle, on his walks, had led me a good number of times:

it is the *Temple of Philosophy*, which its founder had
not had the good fortune of finishing. It has the shape
of the Tiburtine Sibyl's temple, and, still standing under the protection of a thicket of pines, it displays all
the great names of thought, beginning with Mon-
taigne and Descartes, and ending with Rousseau. This
unfinished edifice is already a mere ruin, the creeping
ivy festoons it with grace, the brambles invade the
disjointed walks. There, as a child, I saw celebrations
where girls dressed in white came to receive prizes
for study and good behavior. Where are the rose
bushes that encircled the hill? The dog rose and rasp-
berry bushes hide the last plants, which return to a
wild state. As for the laurel, had someone cut them
down, as in the song about young girls who no longer
want to enter the wood? No, those shrubs of sweet
Italy have perished under our overcast skies. Fortunately Virgil's privet continues to flower, as if to back
up the words of the master inscribed above the door:
Rerum cognoscere causas![6] – Yes, this temple decays
like so many others; men, forgetful or tired, will one
day stop visiting it, indifferent nature will take back
the terrain that art once disputed; but the thirst to
know the reason for things will remain eternal, moving with all force and activity!

Here are the island's poplars, and Rousseau's
tomb, empty of his ashes. O sage! You had given us
the milk of strong men, and we were too weak to
profit from it. We have forgotten your lessons which
our fathers knew, and we have lost the meaning of
your expression, last echo of antique wisdom. But we

---

[6]*Rerum*...: Latin for "know the reason for things." Virgil, *Georgics*,
book II.

will not despair, and as you did at your last moment, we turn our eyes toward the sun!

I saw the chateau again, the placid waters that border it, the falls that groan between the rocks, and that walkway reuniting the two parts of the village, which four dovecotes mark the angles of, the lawn that extends beyond it like a savannah, dominated by the shady hills; Gabrielle's tower is reflected from afar on the waters of the artificial lake studded with ephemeral flowers; the foam bubbles, the insect hums... One must escape the perfidious air that is exhaled there by reaching the powdery greys of the desert and the lands where pink heather offsets the green ferns. How solitary and sad it all is! Sylvie's enchanted expression, her mad walks, her joyous cries, previously added so much charm to the places that I have just walked through! She was still a wild child, her feet bare, her skin suntanned, despite the straw hat, the wide ribbon of which floated pell-mell among her tresses of dark hair. We went to drink milk at the Swiss farm, and someone said to me: "How pretty she is, your girlfriend, little Parisian!" Oh! at that time, a country fellow could not have danced with her! Back then, she danced only with me, once a year, at the celebration of the bow.

Big Curly

I regained the road to Loisy; everyone was awake.
Sylvie's toilette was that of a young lady, nearly in
the style of the city. She had me come up to her room
with all the ingenuousness of before. Her eyes still
sparkled and she had a smile full of charm, but the
pronounced arch of her eyebrows gave her face a serious look at times. Her room was decorated with simplicity, but the furniture was modern, – a gilt framed
mirror had replaced the old pier glass where an idyllic
shepherd was seen offering a bird's nest to a blue and
pink shepherdess. The bed with columns chastely
draped in an old Persian fabric of leafy design had
been replaced by a walnut couchette with an ar-
row-shaped headboard garnished with a curtain; at the
window, in the cage where previously there had been
warblers, there were canaries. I was in a hurry to
leave that room where I found nothing of the past.
"Are you not working at your lace today?..." I said to
Sylvie. "Oh! I don't do lace anymore, nobody asks
for it anymore in the village; even at Chantilly, the
factory is closed." "What do you do then?" She went
to look in the corner of the room for an iron instru-
ment that resembled a long pair of tongs. "What is
that?" "It's what they call the *mechanical*; it's for
holding the skin of gloves in order to sew them."
"Ah! are you glove maker, Sylvie?" "Yes, we work
here for Dammartin, it pays a lot at the moment; but I
am not working today; let's go wherever you like." I
turned my eyes toward the road to Othys; she shook
her head; I understood that her old aunt was no longer
alive. Sylvie called for a boy and had him saddle a

donkey. "I'm still tired from yesterday," she said, "but going out will do me some good; let's go to Chaâlis." And before I knew it, we were traversing the forest, followed by that boy armed with a switch. Soon Sylvie wanted to stop, and I kissed her cheek while helping her down to sit. The conversation between us could no longer be very intimate. I had to tell her about my life in Paris, my trips... "How can anyone go so far away?" she asked. "I'm surprised to see you again." "Oh! that goes without saying!" "And you must admit that you are prettier these days." "I don't know anything about it." "Do you remember the time when we were still children and you were taller?" "And you were more well-behaved!" "Oh! Sylvie!" "They set us on the donkey, each in a basket." "And we didn't use the formal 'vous' with each other... And do you remember when you showed me how to catch crawfish under the bridges of the Thève and Nonette?" "And you, do you remember your milk brother who pulled you *out of the water* one day." "*Big curly*! he was the one who told me I could cross it... *the water!*"

I hastened to change the conversation. This last memory had keenly reminded me of the time when I had first come to the village, dressed in a little outfit in the English style which made the peasants laugh. Sylvie was the only one who found me well-dressed; but I didn't dare remind her of that opinion of so long ago. I don't know why my thoughts brought me back to the wedding outfits we had dressed in at her old aunt's house in Othys. I asked her what happened to them. "Ah! my good aunt," said Sylvie, "had loaned me her dress for the dance at the carnival in Dammartin, two years ago. The next year, she died, my poor aunt!"

She sighed and tears filled her eyes, so much so that I could not ask her under what circumstances she had gone to a masked ball; but, by the grace of her talents as a worker, I understood rather well that Sylvie was no longer the country girl. Her parents alone had remained in their station, and she lived among them like an industrious fairy, dispensing abundance around her.

Return

We could see the view as we exited the woods. We had arrived at the edge of the ponds of Chaâlis. The cloister's galleries, the chapel with slender ogives, the feudal tower and the little chateau that covered up the love affair between Henri IV and Gabrielle was tinged with the red colors of evening on the somber green of the forest. "It's a landscape out of Walter Scott, don't you think?" said Sylvie. "And how do you know about Walter Scott?" I asked her. "You have read a lot of books then in the last three years!... As for myself, I try to forget books, and what charms me is to see this old abbey again with you, where, as children, we hid in the ruins. Do you remember, Sylvie, the fear you felt when the warden told us the story about the red monks?" "Oh! don't remind me." "So sing to me the song of the beautiful girl abducted from her father's garden, under the white rosebush." "I don't sing that anymore." "Would you have become a musician?" "A little." "Sylvie, Sylvie, I'm certain that you sing opera tunes!" "Why are you complaining?" "Because I loved the old tunes, and you will have forgotten how to sing them anymore."

Sylvie modulated several tunes from a famous modern opera... She *phrased!*

We had walked around the neighboring ponds. Here was the green lawn, surrounded by linden trees and elms, where we had often danced! I had the vanity to point out the Carolingian walls and decipher the armorial bearings of the House of Este. "And look at

you! You've read so much more than me!" said
Sylvie. "So you're a scholar now?"

I was piqued by her reproachful tone. Up until
that moment, I had sought the proper place to renew
the moment of expansion from this morning; but what
to say to her with the accompaniment of an donkey
and a very alert boy, who was pleased to draw near in
order to hear a Parisian converse? I made the mistake
at that moment of retelling the story of the apparition
of Chaâlis, which lingered in my memories. I led
Sylvie into the hall of the chateau where I had heard
Adrienne sing even. "Oh! let me hear you sing!" I
said to her; "let your dear voice resonate here under
these vaults and chase away the spirit that torments
me, whether it was divine or fatal!" – She repeated
the words and the song them after me:

Angles, descend promptly
To the bottom of purgatory!...

"That is sad!" she said to me.

"It's sublime... I think it's Porpora,[7] with verses translated in the sixteenth century."

"I don't know," Sylvie responded.

We returned through the valley, following the
road to Charlepont, which the peasants, seldom ety-
mologists by nature, stubbornly called *Chállepont*.
Sylvie, weary of riding on the donkey, leaned on my
arm. The road was deserted; I tried to speak about the
things in my heart, but, I don't know why, I found

---

[7]Porpora: Nicola Porpora (AD 1686 -1768), an Italian composer.

only commonplaces, or all of a sudden some pompous phrase from a novel, which Sylvie might have read. I would stop talking then with a style that was totally classical, and she was surprised sometimes by these interrupted effusions. Having arrived at the walls of Saint S***, we needed to be careful where we stepped. We crossed the wet prairies where the streams meandered. – "What ever happened to the nun?" I asked all of a sudden.

"Ah! You really are terrible with your nun... And well!... and well! that didn't turn out so well."

Sylvie did not wish to say another word.

Do women really feel that this or that expression passes over a person's lips without coming from the heart? One would not think so, to see them so easily abused, to take stock of most of the choices they make most often: there are men who play the comedy of love so well! I have never been able to do so, although being aware that certain women knowingly accept being deceived. Besides, a love that goes as far back as childhood is something sacred... Sylvie, whom I had seen grow up, was like a sister to me. I could not attempt a seduction... An entirely different thought came into my head... – At this time of the day, I said to myself, I would normally be at the theater... I wonder what part Aurélie (that was the name of the actress) must be playing this evening then? Evidently the role of the princess in the new drama. Oh! the third act, how touching she is in it!... And in the love scene of the second! with that young lead with the wrinkled face...

"Are you caught up in your reflections?" said Sylvie, and she began to sing:

In Dammartin there're three beautiful girls:
There's one, more beautiful than the day...

"Ah! how naughty!" I cried, "You see: you do know the old songs still."

"If you came round more often, I would bring out even more of them," she said, "but it's time for a reality check. You have your affairs in Paris, and I have my work; let's not go home too late: I must get up early tomorrow morning."

Father Dodu

I was going to respond, I was going to fall at her feet,
I was going to buy my uncle's house, which it was
still possible for me to do, given there were several
legatees, and that little property had remained jointly
owned; but then we reached Loisy. They all were
waiting for us for supper. The *soupe à l'oignon* emit-
ted its patriarchal odor far and wide. The neighbors
had been invited to that dinner of the day after the
celebration. I immediately recognized an old wood-
cutter, Father Dodu, who used to tell such comical or
such terrible stories in the evenings. Alternately shepherd, messenger, gamekeeper, fisherman, poacher
even, Father Dodu fabricated cuckoo clocks and rotis-
series in his spare time. For a long time now he had
dedicated himself to guiding English visitors to Ermenonville, pointing out Rousseau's meditation spots
and telling them stories about his last days. He was
the little boy whom the philosopher employed to clas-
sify his herbs, and he was the one who received the
order to collect the hemlock that he extracted the sap
from into his cup of *café au lait*. The innkeeper of
The Golden Cross contested that detail with him;
whence the protracted hatreds. Father Dodu had long
been reproached for being in possession of several
quite innocent secrets, like that of curing cows with a
line of verse spoken backwards and making a sign of
the cross drawn with his left foot, but he had renounced those superstitions a long time ago, – thanks
to the memory, he said, of Jean-Jacques' conversa-
tions.

"There you are! little Parisian," said Father Dodu to me. "Have you come to debauch our girls?" "Me, Father Dodu?" "You lead them into the woods when the wolf is not there, isn't that right?" "Father Dodu, it's you who are the wolf." "I was as long as I found sheep; at present, I encounter only goats anymore, and my they sure know how to defend themselves! But you folks in Paris, you are the crafty ones. Jean-Jacques was right when he said: 'A man grows corrupt in the empoisoned air of the cities.'" "Father Dodu, you know perfectly well that men grow corrupt everywhere."

Father Dodu began to sing a drinking song; we wanted to stop him before a certain scabrous couplet that everyone knew by heart, but it was pointless. Sylvie did not want to sing, despite our encouragements, saying that one did not sing at the table. I had already noticed that her lover from the evening before was seated to her left. He had something, I don't know what, in his round face, in his tousled hair, that I recognized. He got up and came to stand behind my chair saying: "So you don't recognize me, Parisian?" A good woman who had just returned to her dessert after having served us, said into my ear: "You don't recognize your milk brother?" Without that warning, I was going to be ridiculous. "Ah! it's you, *big frizzy!*" I said, "it's you, the one who pulled me out of the *water!*" Sylvie burst out laughing at that recognition. "Not to mention," said the boy who embraced me, "that you had a beautiful silver watch on you, that you were more concerned about the watch than your person, because it stopped working; you said: 'the *animal* is *drown'd*, it no longer goes tick-tock; what will my uncle say?..."'

"An animal in the watch!" said Father Dodu, "the things they teach children in Paris!"

Sylvie was feeling sleepy, I figured I was no longer on her mind. She went up to her room, and as I kissed her cheeks, she said: "See you tomorrow, come by and see us!"

Father Dodu had remained seated at the table with Sylvain and my milk brother; we talked for a long time over a flask of *ratafiat* from Lourdes. "All men are equal," said Father Dodu between two cou-plets, "I drink with a pastry cook same as I would with a prince." "Where is the pastry cook?" I asked. "Look next to you! a young man who aspires to set himself up."

My milk brother looked embarrassed. Now I understood everything. It was my fate to have a milk brother in the countryside made famous by Rousseau, – who wanted to suppress wet nurses! Father Dodu informed me that Sylvie most likely was going to marry the *big frizzy*, who was planning to set up a pastry shop in Dammartin. I didn't ask any more questions. The Nanteuil-le-Haudoin carriage brought me back to Paris on the following day.

Aurélie

Paris! The carriage ride took five hours. My only concern was to arrive in the evening. Towards eight o'-clock, I was seated in my usual box seat; Aurélie infused her inspiration and charm into verses feebly inspired by Schiller, which was the work of a person of mediocre talent of the time. In the scene in the garden, she was sublime. During the fourth act, which she did not appear in, I went to buy a bouquet of flowers at Madame Prévost's. I inserted a very tender letter signed: *A stranger*. I said to myself: There, something fixed for the future; and on the following day, I was on the road to Germany.

What was I going to do there? To try and put some order to my emotions. If I were writing a novel, I would never have been able to make people believe a story about one heart taken with two lovers simultaneously. It was my own fault that Sylvie was escaping me; but having seen her for just one day was enough to lift my soul: I placed her from then on on a pedestal like a smiling statue in the Temple of Wisdom. Seeing her had pulled me back from the brink. I had even greater strength to resist the thought of going up to Aurélie and introducing myself, only to struggle with so much vulgar amorousness that shined one moment, as I stood beside her, and fell to pieces the next. "One day we'll see," I said to myself, "if that woman has a heart."

One morning I read in a journal that Aurélie was ill. I wrote to her from the Salzburg hills. The letter was so embued with German mysticism that I had no reason to expect much success, but I also did not ask for a reply. I counted a little on chance and on – the *stranger*.

Months passed. Between my outings and my leisure time, I had undertaken to fix in a poetic drama the love of the painter Colonna for the beautiful Laura, whose parents had made her a religious, and whom he loved to the end. Something in that story reminded me of my constant preoccupations. Having written the last verse of the drama, I was no longer thinking of returning to France.

What can I say that isn't the story of countless others? I passed through all the circles of those places of trial called theaters. "I have eaten the drum and drunk the cymbal," as we say in French, lacking in any apparent understanding of the Eleusinian initiations. It means doubtless that one must go beyond the limits of nonsense and absurdity: for me it meant I needed to conquer and fix my ideal.

Aurélie had accepted the principal role in the drama that I had brought back from Germany. I will never forget the day when she permitted me to read the piece to her. The scenes of love were written with her in mind. I do believe that I recited them with soul, but above all enthusiasm. In the conversation that followed, I revealed myself as the *stranger* of the two letters. She said to me: "You are quite mad: but come see me again... I have never found anyone who knew how to love me."

O woman! you look for love... And what

about me?

In the days that followed, I wrote to her the most tender letters, the most beautiful letters doubtless that she had ever received. I received from her in response letters full of reason. For a moment she was touched, summoned me to her, and confessed to me that it was difficult for her to break a previous attachment. "If it is really *for me* that you love me," she said, "you will understand that my heart can only belong to one person."

Two months later, I received a letter full of effusion. I ran to her. Someone gave me a precious detail in the meantime. The handsome young man whom I had run into one night at the circle had just accepted a position in the Spahi.

The following summer, there were trips to Chantilly. The theater troupe that Aurélie acted in gave a representation there. Once in the country, the troupe was for three days at the stage manager's command. I made a friend of that good man, the old Dorante of the Marivaux comedies, the young lead for a long time, and whose last success had been the role of the lover in the piece imitating Schiller, where my opera glasses had shown him to be so wrinkled. Up close, he appeared younger, and, having remained slender, he still left an impression in the provinces. He had passion. I accompanied the troupe in the capacity of *lord poet*; I persuaded the stage manager to go and give performances in Senlis and Dammartin. He was leaning at first toward Compiègne; but Aurélie was of my same opinion. On the following day, while they were busy with the proprietors of the hall and the authorities, I rented some horses and we took the road around the lakes of Commelle in order to lunch at the chateau of Queen Blanche. Aurélie, as an Amazon, with her blond hair floating in the wind, traversed the forest like a queen of olde, and the peasants stopped to look, astonished. – Madame de F*** was the only person they would have seen before so imposing and so graceful in her greetings. After lunch, we went down to the villages that are reminiscent of Switzerland, where the water of the Nonette made the mills turn. Those aspects dear to my memory interested her but without arresting her attention. I was planning to bring Aurélie to the chateau, near Orry, over the same green sward where I had seen Adrienne for the first time. – She showed no emotion. Then I told her everything; I told her about the source of that love glimpsed during the night, dreamed about later, realized in her. She listened to me seriously and said: "You don't love me! You are waiting for me to say: The actress is the same as the nun; you are looking for a drama, and there you have it, and the denouement evades you. Go away, I no longer believe you!"

Her words were a revelation to me. Those bizarre enthusiasms that I had felt so long ago, those dreams, those tears, those despairs, and those tender feelings... they were not love, then? But where is love then?

Aurélie performed that night in Senlis. I thought I could detect that she had a weakness for the stage manager, – the young wrinkled lead actor. That man was an excellent person and had assisted her.

Aurélie said to me one day: "The man who loves me, behold!"

Last Page

Such are the chimeras that charm and distract the mind in the morning of life. I have tried to fix them without much order, but plenty of hearts will understand me. The illusions fall one after the other, like the skin of a fruit, and the fruit is experience. Its taste is bitter; it has something acrid however that fortifies, – I wish only that people might forgive me for this old-fashioned style of mine. Rousseau says that the scenes of nature console everything. I search sometimes to find my copses of Clarens lost to the north of Paris, in the fog. All that has completely changed!

Ermenonville! country where the ancient idyll still flourished, – translated a second time in the style of Gessner! You have lost your only star, which shimmered for me doubly bright. Alternately blue and pink like the deceptive star of Aldebaran, it was Adrienne or Sylvie, – it was the two halves of a single love. The one was a sublime ideal, the other was sweet reality. What can your shadows and your lakes do for me now, or even your desert? Othys, Montagny, Loisy, poor neighboring hamlets, Chaâlis, – which is being restored, – you have retained nothing of all that past! Sometimes, I need to revisit these places of solitude and revery. Sadly, I notice in myself the fugitive traces of an epoch wherein the natural was affected; I smile at times on reading on the face of granite certain verses by Roucher, which appeared sublime to me, – or charitable maxims above a fountain or grotto sacred to Pan. The ponds, crossed at such great effort, spread in vain their dead water which the swan disdains. Those days are gone when hunting parties from Condé passed with their proud Amazons, when their horns responded from afar, multiplied by the echoes!... To arrive at Ermenonville, there is no longer a direct route today. Sometimes I go there via Creil and Senlis, other times via Dammartin.

One arrives at Dammartin only in the evening. I will stay the night at the *Image Saint-Jean*. I am ordinarily given a fairly clean room hung with old tapestries and a pier glass over the window. That room is a last return to the bric-à-brac that I have renounced for so long a time now. One sleeps warmly under the eiderdown, which is customary in those parts. In the morning, when I open the window, bordered by vines and roses, I am ravished to discover a green horizon of ten leagues in length, where the poplars line up like armies. Some villages take shelter here and there under their pointed steeples, constructed, as it was said then, in points made of bone. Othys can be made out first, – then Ève, then Ver; Ermenonville would be seen through the woods, if it had a steeple, – but in that philosophical place the church has been rather neglected. After having filled my lungs with the exceptionally pure air that one respires on those plateaus, I descend gaily and will pay a visit to the pastry cook. "There you are, big frizzy!" "There you are, little Parisian!" We give each other friendly punches in the arm as we have since childhood, then I climb a certain staircase where the joyful cries of two children welcome my arrival. The Athenian smile of Sylvie brightens her charming features. I tell myself: "This was happiness perhaps, and yet..."

I sometimes call her Lolotte, and she finds that I resemble Werther a little, without the pistols, which are no longer fashionable. While the great frizzy is busy with his lunch, we go to take the children for a stroll along the linden-tree lined paths that encircle the debris of the old brick towers of the chateau. While the children practice, drawing the bows of their companions, embedding their father's arrows in the straw, we read some poetry or several pages of those very short books that nobody makes anymore.

I forgot to mention that the day the troupe that Aurélie was a member of gave their performance in Dammartin, I brought Sylvie to the show, and I asked her if the actress did not look like someone she knew before. "Who?" "You remember Adrienne?"

She burst out laughing and said: "What an idea!" Then, as if to reproach herself, she sighed: "Poor Adrienne! she died in the convent of Saint-S***, in 1832."

The Chimeras

El Desdichado[8]

I am the tenebrous, – the widower, – the disconsolate
Prince of Aquitaine in a ruined tower:
My only *star* is dead, – and my lute, constellated,
Bears the *black sun* of *Melancholy*.

In the dark night of the tomb, you who consoled me,
Grant me the Posillipo and the sea of Italy,
The *flower* that so pleased my heart which is desolate,
And the trellis where vines with roses intertwine.

Am I Eros or Phoebus, Lusignan or Byron?
My face still blushes from the kiss of the queen;
I have dreamed in the grotto where swims the siren...

And, twice the victor, I have crossed the Acheron:
Modulating alternately on Orpheus' lyre
The sighs of the saint and the cries of the faery.

    – 1853.

---

[8]*El Desdichado*: Spanish for "the dispossessed" or "the disinherited."

Myrtho

I think of you, Myrto, divine enchantress,
Of lofty Posillipo, with its thousand glimmering fires,
Of your face inundated by Eastern lights,
And dark grapes entangled in your golden tresses.

It is from your cup too that I drank drunkeness,
And in the furtive flashes of your smiling eye,
When at Iacchus' feet you saw me praying to
          goddesses,
For the Muse made me one of Greece's sons.

I know why the volcano acted up again...
Yesterday you touched it with your foot,
And suddenly cinders covered the horizon,

Ever since a Norman duke smashed your clay gods,
Forever, beneath Virgil's boughs of laurel,
Pale Hortensia unites with green Myrtle!

    – *1854.*

Horus

The god Kneph, trembling, shook the universe;
Then Isis, his mother, rose up in bed,
Made a hateful gesture at her ferocious spouse,
And in her green eyes her former ardor blazed.

"Do you see him," she said, "he dies, that perverse
          old man,
All the world's winter has passed through his mouth,
Bind his twisted foot, spend his shady eye,
He's the god of volcanoes, the king of winters!

"The eagle has passed, a new spirit calls me,
I have donned the Sibyl's dress for him...
Beloved child of Hermes and Osiris!"

Then the goddess fled on her golden conch,
The sea reflected her adored image to us,
And heaven shone under the scarf of Iris.

Anteros

You ask why I have so much rage at heart
And an indomitable head on a pliant neck:
I was born of the race of Antaeus,
And the victorious god's arrows I deflect.

Yes, I am one of those whom the Avenger inspires,
He marked my forehead with his angry lips,
Under Abel's bloodied pallor, alas!
At times I wear Cain's implacable red face!

Jehovah! the last, vanquished by your genie,
Who, from the depths of hell, cried: "O tyranny!"
He is my forebear Belus, or my father Dagon...

They dipped me in the waters of Cocytus thrice,
And, protecting my Amalekite mother on my own,
I resow at her feet the teeth of the old dragon.

Delphica

Ultima Cumæi venit jam carminis ætas.

Do you know that ancient ballad, Daphne,
At the foot of the sycamore, under the white laurels,
Under the olive tree, the myrtle, or quaking aspens,
That love song... that always repeats?

Do you recognize the temple, with its huge peristyle,
Bitter lemons with the marks of your teeth?
And the grotto, fatal to imprudent hosts,
Where the ancient seed of the defeated dragon sleeps.

Those gods you weep for today, – they will return!
Time will restore the order of bygone days;
The earth shivered on account of a prophetic breeze...

But the Sibyl with her Latin face
Is asleep under the Arch of Constantine:
And nothing has disturbed the austere portico.

– 1843, Tivoli.

Artemis

The Thirteenth returns... it is still the first;
And it is always the one, – or the only moment:
For are you, queen, o you! the first or last?
And are you, king, the only or the last lover?

Love the one who loved you, from cradle to worms;
The woman I loved still loves me tenderly:
It is death – or the deceased – O delight! O torment!
The rose she holds, it is the *Alcea rosea*.

Neapolitan saint with your hands filled with fire,
Rose with the violet heart, Saint Gudula's flower;
Have you found your cross in the desert of the skies?

White roses, fall! You insult our gods;
Fall, white phantoms, from your burning heaven; –
The saint of the abyss is holier in my eyes!

Christ in the Garden of Olives

(In imitation of Jean Paul)

> *God is dead! The sky is empty...*
> *Weep! children, you no longer have a father!*
>   – Jean Paul

I.

When the Lord, lifting his thin arms to the sky,
Beneath the sacred trees, as poets pretend,
Was long lost in silent sorrow,
And felt betrayed by ungrateful friends;

He turned to those waiting at his feet
Dreaming to be kings, sages, prophets...
But they were torpid, sleeping soundly like beasts,
And he began to cry: "No, God does not exist!"

They slept. "Friends, have you heard the *news?*
I touched with my head the eternal vault;
I am bloody, broken, suffering for many days!

Brothers, I deceived you. Abyss, abyss, abyss!
God is missing from the altar, where I'm the victim...
God does not exist! He's dead!" But they slept!

II.

He resumed: "All is dead! I traversed worlds;
And I lost myself in flight, in milky ways,
So distant that life, in its fecund veins,
Expends golden sands and silver waves.

"Everywhere the deserted ground bordered by waves,
The confused tourbillons of agitated oceans...
A vague breeze the vagabond spheres moves,
But no spirit exists in those immensities.

"While looking for the eye of God, I saw an orbit,
Vast, dark, and bottomless, where the night that
              inhabits it
Shines on the world, and ever thicker grows;

"A strange rainbow surrounds that somber well,
Sill of ancient chaos whose emptiness is darkness,
A spiral, engulfing days and worlds!"

III.

"Implacable Destiny, silent sentinel,
Cold Necessity!... Hazard that as it gains on you,
Among dead worlds beneath eternal snows,
Refrigerates, by degrees, the universe that grows pale.

"Do you know what you're doing, primordial power,
With your spent suns, crushing each other...
Are you certain to convey an immortal breath
Between a dying world and one that's born?

"O my father! Is it you that I feel within me?
Do you have the power to live and defeat death?
Would you have succumbed after a last effort

"By that angel of nights struck by anathema...
For I feel so alone, weeping and suffering,
And if I die, alas! everything dies with me!"

IV.

No one heard the eternal victim groan,
Spilling his heart to the world, in vain;
But, nearly faint and bent over for inanition,
He called out to the only *one* awake in Solyme:

"Judas!" he cried, "You know that people esteem me,
Hurry up and sell me, and end this traffic:
I am suffering, friend! lying on the ground...
Come on! you who, at least, have the strength for
        crime!"

But Judas walked away malcontent and pensive,
Feeling himself ill paid, full of a remorse so vivid
That he read his dark state of mind on all the walls.

Finally Pilate, alone, who was serving Caesar,
Feeling some pity, turned around as chance would
        have it:
"Go find that fool!" he told his satellite.

V.

It was him indeed, that fool, that sublime madman...
That forgotten Icarius who mounted the skies,
That Phaethon struck by the gods' thunderbolts,
That comely, murdered Atys whom Cybele
          resurrects!

The augur interrogated the victim's flank,
The earth was drunk on his precious blood...
The universe, teetering on its axles, was stunned,
And Olympus tottered and nearly tanked.

"Answer!" cried Caesar to Jupiter Ammon,
"Who is this new god being erected on earth?
And, if he's not a god, he must be a demon..."

But the oracle invoked forever had to stop;
For one entity alone could explain that mystery:
He who gave a soul to the children of clay.

– 1844.

Golden Verses

Eh, what! All things are sentient!
– Pythagorus

Man, free thinker! Do you think you are the only one
Who thinks in a world abounding in life?
Your freedom disposes the forces you possess,
But the universe is absent in all your advice.

Respect an active mind in animals:
Every flower is a blossoming soul to Nature;
A mystery of love inhabits metal;
"All things are sentient!" All have the power
        to impact you.

In a blind wall that watches you, beware the eye:
Every element of matter has a name...
Do not let it serve an act of impiety!

In an obscure being, a god is often hidden;
And, like a nascent eye covered by its lid,
A pure spirit grows beneath a rock's outer skin!

    – 1845.

The Armed Head

Napoleon, dying, saw an *Armed head*...
He thought about his son, feeble and suffering;
The Head, it was his beloved France, decapitated,
At the feet of the Caesar who was expiring.

God, who judged that man and his renown,
Recalled his son, Jesus Christ; and the opening hole
Expelled but an empty breath, a specter of smoke:
The demi-god, defeated, rose greater than before.

So a young man inundated with the tears of Victory
Was seen exiting the depths of Purgatory,
Offering to heaven's monarchs his pure hand;

Both were, by a double mystery, wounded in the side:
The one spilled his blood, the earth to fecundate,
The other scattered divine seeds in heaven's gate!

Appendix

Gérard de Nerval[9]

... But, more and more, Gérard de Nerval is possessed by that restlessness, that desire to move, to escape men, and to escape himself which plagues great
melancholics and so strongly possessed Watteau, that
other genial enchanter, like a brother to him, towards
the end of his life. – The strange ardor of his gaze re-
veals the intensity of his cerebral combustion. Despite
his extravagant looks, he always maintains his friend-
ships because of the charm of his gentle character and
people's interest in his lucid and transcendent conversation. One evening, in the street, while walking for
several moments with his eyes fixed on a star, he
stops, gets undressed, throws his clothes on the
ground about him, then extends his arms, and waits,
unmoving, until the moment when his soul might
leave his body, "magnetically attracted in the star's
beam of light." A police patrol pulls him out of his
ecstasy and puts him in the slammer. He is seen "running over the ground, flapping his arms like wings."
His reason continues to be clouded. During the day,
he is prey to hallucinations: his nights are peopled
with nightmares. Work becomes difficult for him. On
many occasions, he wants to suicide. Two times, in
1853, he is forced to go into recovery under the care
of Dr. Blanche,[10] then at the house in Dubois. It is on

---

[9]This is an excerpt from "Gérard de Nerval" a biography by Henri
Strentz in issue no. 44 of *Portraits d'hier*, a bi-monthly
publication, January 1, 1911, Paris.

[10]Dr. Blanche: Émile Blanche (AD 1820-1893) a French psychi-
atrist and the friend of many artists of his day.

his exit from this last that he writes *Sylvie*, his master-piece, that so resplendent miracle of elegiac and moving French sensibility. Several days after its publication in the *Revue des Deux-Mondes*, Gérard is seized, in the street, by so furious a mental breakdown that he is led to the nearest hospital and put into a straitjacket; he is later transferred back into Dr. Blanche's care. This is no longer the happy dementia of his first crisis; a dark sadness consumes him. As soon as he is released, he departs for Germany. He returns to Paris only to go and stay once again at the house in Passy;[11] but soon, in response to his supplications, he is released. He departs for Germany again. From a letter addressed to a friend, it emerges that despite the joyful distractions that he seeks in that country, his mental sufferings have not stopped and his anxiety about his creative faculties obsesses him.

In 1854, the *Filles du Feu* appears. The disorder of his life as a poet is at its height now. He no longer has a fixed domicile, and works on the tables in cabarets; he lodges at dives. It is in this state of moral anguish that, with the assistance of sorrowful, painful, or enchanting images seen during diverse fits of madness, impressions from what he calls "his second life," he composes *Aurélia, or Dream and Life*, a sort of autobiography wherein he attempted, he says, to "transcribe the impressions of a long illness that transpired entirely within the mysteries of my mind." A singular work, serene and heart-rending, which Gérard de Nerval himself calls, with stupefying tran-

---

[11]House in Passy: a quarter in Paris where Dr. Blanche had another clinic.

quility, the effusion of dream into real life, but which Théophile Gautier more accurately qualified as: Rational Thought writing the memories of his Madness under its dictation. A ruthless journal of Gérard de Nerval's last battle between his real *me* and his mystical *me* amidst the unfortunate circumstances of a passion that killed him. The first part of it appeared in the *Revue de Paris*, January 1, 1855.

A most tragic existence occupies the last days of the poet's life. It is winter, a hard winter; the snow falls constantly. Ice floes runs noisily into the piles of the bridges spanning the Seine. Dressed only in a thin black habit, Gérard de Nerval, abandoned to an exaltation that alone prevents him from trembling because of the cold, wanders about the city, fleeing the illness that will finally take him. In front of his friends, at his wit's end, in strange improvisations, his beautiful intelligence dazzles them for the last time.

On January 20, he takes out from his pocket, in front of Théophile Gautier and Maxime Du Camp, the apron string: "This is the belt that Mme. de Maintenon wore when she played *Esther* at Saint-Cyr," he assures them.[12] On the 24th, he writes to one of his friends: "Come find me at Châtelet." He had spent the night in a dive at Les Halles, and is picked up by the police in a roundup of vagabonds. – "I'm lucky if I can write twenty lines a day," he confesses in another letter, "so great is the darkness that closes in on me..." A terrible confession that forever shines a light on the mystery of his last days.

---

[12]*Esther*: a tragedy written by Jean Racine and performed for the first time on January 26, 1689, at St. Cyr.

On the night of January 25, at around three o'-
clock in the morning, close to Châtelet, he sets out by
entering the horrible and fetid small rue de la Vieille
Lanterne,[13] demolished since then, which leads by a
stair of twelve sticky steps to another no less frighten-
ing path: the rue de la Tuerie.[14] The cold is intense,
his solitude ghastly, and snow covers the ground.
Gérard, scantily dressed as usual, stops in front of a
night shelter where he has often found a place to stay.
He knocks at the door for a long time. Is everyone
asleep inside? Is there no more room? Nobody re-
sponds.

Several hours later, at the break of dawn, truck
farmers returning from Les Halles discover the
hanged body. A string – the apron string that he had
displayed as Mme. de Maintenon's belt – bound his
head, gentle and chimerical, to a bar of the window,
just below the key that served as a business sign for
the key shop, and next to a sewer drain. His feet
brushed the pavement. And, so that nothing "Ner-
valian" was lacking from this dreadful scene, it is said
how a crow, which seemed like a "double" of the one
that the poet had seen on the bridge of the boat that
carried him to Syria, hopped up the steps of the dirty
stairs, cawing, sinisterly, the two single words that it
knew: "j'ai soif!"[15]

---

[13]Rue de la Vieille Lanterne: French for "Old Lantern Street."

[14]Rue de la Tuerie: French for "Slaughter Street."

[15]J'ai soif: French for "I'm thirsty."

Other Books by the Publisher

Fanchette's Pretty Little Foot by Restif de La Bretonne

Je M'Accuse... by Léon Bloy

My Hospitals & My Prisons by Paul Verlaine

Salvation Through the Jews by Léon Bloy

Words of a Demolitions Contractor by Léon Bloy

Cellulely by Paul Verlaine

Ecclesiastical Laurels by Jacques Rochette de la Morlière

Flowers of Bitumen by Émile Goudeau

Songs for Her & Odes in Her Honor by Paul Verlaine

On Huysmans' Tomb by Léon Bloy

Ten Years a Bohemian by Émile Goudeau

The Soul of Napoleon by Léon Bloy

Blood of the Poor by Léon Bloy

Joan of Arc and Germany by Léon Bloy

A Platonic Love by Paul Alexis

The Revealer of the Globe: Christopher Columbus & His Future Beatification (Part One) by Léon Bloy

An Immodest Proposal by Dr. Helmut Schleppend

The Pornographer by Restif de La Bretonne

Style (Theory and History) by Ernest Hello

On the Threshold of the Apocalypse: 1913-1915 by Léon Bloy

She Who Weeps (Our Lady of La Salette) by Léon Bloy

The Sylph by Claude Prosper Jolyot de Crébillon (*fils*)

Voyage in France by a Frenchman by Paul Verlaine

Ourigan, Oregon by William Clark, Richard Robinson, and anonymous

Drowning by Yu Dafu

Cull of April by Francis Vielé-Griffin

The Misfortune of Monsieur Fraque by Paul Alexis

Fêtes Galantes & Songs Without Words by Paul Verlaine

Joys by Francis Vielé-Griffin

The Son of Louis XVI by Léon Bloy

Septentrion by Jean Raspail

The Resurrection of Villiers de l'Isle-Adam by Léon Bloy

Poems Saturnian by Paul Verlaine

The Biography of Léon Bloy: Memories of a Friend by René Martineau

Fredegund, France: A Book of Poetry by Richard Robinson

The Good Song by Paul Verlaine

Swans by Francis Vielé-Griffin

Constantinople and Byzantium by Léon Bloy

Enamels and Cameos by Théophile Gautier

Four Years of Captivity in Cochons-sur-Marne: 1900-1904 by Léon Bloy

Dark Minerva: Prolegomena: The Moral Construction of Dante's Divine Comedy by Giovanni Pascoli

What is Fascism: Discourses and Polemics by Giovanni Gentile

The Desperate Man by Léon Bloy

Meditations of a Solitary in 1916 by Léon Bloy

The Ride of Yeldis & Other Poems by Francis Vielé-Griffin